CHLOË AND MAUDE

ME

MAUDE

LITTLE, BROWN AND COMPANY
BOSTON • TORONTO

FIRST EDITION

A version of the story "The Art Lesson" first appeared in the
November 1983 issue of Redbook.

Library of Congress Cataloging in Publication Data
Boynton, Sandra.
    Chloë and Maude.
    Contents: The art lesson – Chloë, Maude, and Sophia –
Overnight.
    1. Children's stories, American. [1. Cats – Fiction.
2. Friendship – Fiction] I. Title.
PZ7.B6968Ch 1985   [E]   85-161
ISBN 0-316-10492-2
ISBN 0-316-10491-4 (pbk.)

AHS

Published simultaneously in Canada
by Little, Brown & Company (Canada) Limited

Contents

Story Number One

THE ART LESSON

Chloë loved to draw.
She drew magical castles

and angry dancing dragons.

She drew trains with lots and lots of cars.

She drew spaghetti,

her friend Maude,

families,

forests

and elephants.

Chloë's friend Maude
did not like to draw.

3

"But Maude," said Chloë, "you draw very well. Just look at this nice jump rope you made!"

"THAT'S SUPPOSED TO BE A SNAKE!" said Maude, "AND I'M GOING HOME —

"AND I'M NEVER GOING
TO MAKE ANOTHER PICTURE
AS LONG AS I LIVE
AND I DON'T CARE
IF EVERYONE THINKS
YOU'RE SO GREAT
JUST BECAUSE
YOUR PICTURES LOOK
LIKE WHAT
THEY'RE
SUPPOSED
TO, SO
GOOD BYE!"

but she wasn't watching where she was
going and —

this is what happened:

RUN RUN RUN RUN TRIP!

roll roll roll

ah-ah-ah-ah-BOOM!

"WOW!" said Chloë.
"Look at that great painting you made!
I could never do anything
that dramatic!"

"Let's make more paintings!"
said Maude.

So all morning long, while Chloë drew
dragons and castles and trains and
Maude and spaghetti and forests and
families and elephants

and wizards

and other things,

Maude painted *Adagio in Green,*

Sunset in Motion, and

Color Calypso.

And after lunch, they worked together.

Story Number Two

CHLOË, MAUDE AND SOPHIA

Chloë couldn't find Maude
anywhere.

She was not in her room.

She was not in her yard.

She was not in her fort.

"Maude!"
yelled Chloë
inside.

No answer.

"Maude!"
yelled Chloë
outside.

No answer.

16

"MAUDE!
WHERE ARE YOU?"

"There's no Maude living here," said a voice from the driveway.

Chloë looked.

There was Maude, sitting in the back seat of her mother's car, wearing very fancy clothes and reading a very fancy magazine.

"Maude!" said Chloë.
"I've been looking everywhere for you!
What are you doing there?"

"There is no Maude living here any more," said Maude.

"What!" said Chloë. "Are you moving?"

"No," replied Maude,
"I still live here, but
I'm no longer Maude.
It's a plain name and I don't like it.
From now on, I'm going to
call myself 'Sophia'."

"But Maude," said Chloë.

Maude went back to reading her magazine.

"MAUDE!" said Chloë. Maude kept reading.

Chloë sighed. "Sophia?" she said.

"Yes?" said Maude.

"Sophia," said Chloë,
"I came over to ask Maude if she
wanted to go for a hike.
But since she's not here,
would you like to come instead?"

"No, thank you,"
replied Maude.
"Sophias don't hike."

"Well,"
said Chloë,
"Chloës do.
    See you later."

23

The next day, Chloë asked Maude
to come ride bikes, but Maude said,
"Sophias don't bike,"

and Chloë had to go alone.

The next day, Chloë asked Maude
to come bake cookies, but Maude said,
"Sophias don't bake,"

and Chloë made cookies alone.

The day after that,
Chloë didn't call at all.

On the following day, a package
came. The label on it said:

FOR MAUDE

Not to be opened by anyone

except Maude even if your

name used to be Maude but

isn't any more.

Maude didn't know what to do. She wanted to be Sophia. But she couldn't find out what was in the package unless she was Maude.

At last she said, "I'll just put it inside in case Maude comes back." She put it on the hall table,

then went to the drawing room for tea.

At tea, Maude entertained many
important visitors from all over the world.

But somehow she was bored.

Somehow it wasn't fun today,
being Sophia.

Maude went back to look at the package. She thought and thought and thought.

Then at last she decided.

"I'm back!" said Maude. "And look — here's a package for me!"

Quickly she unwrapped it. Inside was a present with another note:

Dear Maude,
    You opened this package, so you must have come back. WELCOME HOME!! I've missed you terribly.
        Love,
        Chloë

Maude opened the present. She took out a handmade  backpack, just like Chloë's, only blue.

"It's beautiful!" cried Maude. "Sophia would hate it, but I think it's the most wonderful present ever!"

Maude ran over to Chloë's house.
"Chloë!" she called. "Chloë!"

Chloë opened her door.

"Oh — hello, Sophia," she said.

"No, no, it's me: Maude!" said
Maude. "See?" She showed Chloë her
backpack.

"You've come back!" cried Chloë,

and she hugged Maude
as hard as she could.

"Let's go hiking!" said Maude.

And so they did.

Story Number Three

OVERNIGHT

Maude came to Chloë's house to spend the night.

First they had dinner at their own special table.

Then they played  Scary Monsters

until it was time to get ready

for bed.

Chloë and Maude tested the bed to make sure it was soft, then they climbed under the covers.

"Good night, Maude," said Chloë, and she turned out the light.

"Good night, Chloë," said Maude.

.   .   .   .

"WHAT WAS THAT?" said Maude.

"What was what?" asked Chloë.

"That whirring and gurgling noise, like...like a monster swallowing!"

Chloë listened a minute. Then she turned the light back on.

"That's just the washing machine,"
Chloë said. "Do you need a night light?"

"Yes," said Maude. "Please."

Chloë went and turned on her little desk lamp

then she climbed back into bed, and turned the big light back off.

"Good night again, Maude," she said. "Sleep well."

"Good night, Chloë," said Maude.

Soon Chloë was fast asleep.

Maude was staring at the ceiling.

The ceiling had a crack in it.
It looked like a crack for a while, then it
started looking like a mouth.

"If I keep watching it," thought
Maude, "then it can't get me. As long
as I don't shut my eyes, I'm safe."

Maude stared at the crack for about
fifty hundred hours.

Then her eyes slowly closed.

Suddenly, Maude realized that she had stopped watching. She sat up and yelled,

"NO, YOU CAN'T GET ME, I'M STILL AWAKE!"

"What what what?"
said Chloë.
"What? Who's that? What?"

"Chloë! It's me — Maude!
I've been guarding you so
you'll be safe, but I almost
fell asleep and it
nearly got us!"

"WHAT nearly got us?" asked Chloë.

"The ceiling."

"WHAT?!"

"That crack is a mouth," explained Maude. "See?"

"Now listen, Maude," said Chloë, "you are being ridiculous. I'M tired and YOU must be tired and there are NO monsters and NO mouths in the ceiling. Now we HAVE TO GO TO SLEEP. RIGHT?"

Maude said, "I'm sorry, Chloë. You're right. I'm really sorry. I'll go right to sleep now. Good night."

Maude lay down, and soon Chloë
heard her lightly snoring.

Now the house seemed very, very
quiet. Chloë looked out the window.
It was very, very dark.

Chloë lay back and pulled up the covers. She closed her eyes.

She opened them again.

"You know," she thought, "Maude was right. That crack really does look like a mouth."

"Maude?" Chloë whispered. "Maude? Are you awake?"

Maude didn't answer.

Chloë didn't know what to do.
She was too tired to stay awake,
and too scared to go to sleep.

"Well," thought Chloë, "if I don't want that crack to be a mouth, I'll just have to change it."

She closed her eyes and imagined herself painting. First she added green to make a hill.

Then she painted in a river and a lake.

Now Chloë imagined that she added a rainbow, some trees, three birds and a setting sun.

Finally, she put in two friends climbing the hill.

By Chloë

"There," thought Chloë. "It's done. My picture is called *Chloë and Maude*."

And then she fell asleep.